Enoch the Emu

Written by Gordon Winch
Illustrated by Doreen Gristwood

Gareth Stevens Publishing
Milwaukee

A long, long time ago
in the far Australian outback
and in the middle of a dusty plain
lived an emu called Enoch.

Enoch was good at eating,
and he was good at kicking,
and he was good at strutting about
with his head in the air.

Enoch's h

2

Emu Club

3

Emu Club
men only

And he was very good at meeting
his friends at the Emu Club,
where he drank too much billabong water.

5

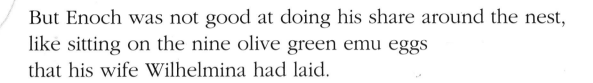

But Enoch was not good at doing his share around the nest,
like sitting on the nine olive green emu eggs
that his wife Wilhelmina had laid.

"I am sick of you, Enoch," she said one night
when he returned home late from the Emu Club.
"I am sick of your no-good ways.
You never take a turn on the nest.
You never bring me a fat juicy grasshopper.
You never ever drum me a little song
as you used to before the eggs came along."

"I am sick of you, Enoch.
I am sick of sitting here
by myself on our eggs.
So! Sit on them yourself
or there will be no babies
for you to boast about
down at the Emu Club!"

And with that Wilhelmina stood up
and flounced past Enoch,
who slumped to the ground
with his mouth wide open in amazement.

Enoch looked at the eggs
as Wilhelmina disappeared down the track.
"HUH!" he said. "What a fuss
about a little bit of egg sitting!
I, Enoch Emu, will show my wife
how easy it is to sit on a clutch of eggs.
I will sit here quietly
until she comes back,
and I won't complain once."

11

So Enoch sat and sat,
but Wilhelmina did not return.
Not all that day, or the next.
Enoch started to get thirsty
and hungry and cramped
and very, very lonely.

13

Then he saw Wilhelmina coming along the track.
"AHA!" he said. "And about time, too!"

"Not so fast, my fine-feathered friend,"
Wilhelmina replied. "Not so fast.
I am here only to tell you that I am off
for a little holiday with my friends.
I'll be back when the eggs are hatched."

15

"But, but, but," spluttered Enoch.
"I'm h-h-hungry and I'm th-th-thirsty.
What a-b-b-bout my lunch?
Come baaaaaaaack!"

But Wilhelmina had really gone this time,
and Enoch was left sitting
all alone
on the nine olive green eggs
in the nest
in the middle of the dusty plain.

Enoch sat and sat
day after day
and week after week
with a look of determination on his face.

No one came near him
except for a bedraggled dingo,
but the wild dog fled
when he saw the fierce look
in Enoch's eye.

He started to lose weight.
His face got thinner and his body got thinner.
His feathers lost their shine.
But still he sat and sat and sat.

Until one morning he heard a strange sound.
PECK! PECK! PECK!
CHEEP! CHEEP! CHEEP!
PECK! PECK! PECK!
CHEEP! CHEEP! CHEEP!
Then he felt something move,
and a tiny, striped head
popped out from under the feathers.

"Hooray!" shouted Enoch.
"I've done it. I'm a dad."
And he drummed with pride
as more emu chicks
poked out their tiny heads.
1 2 3 4 5 6 7 8 9

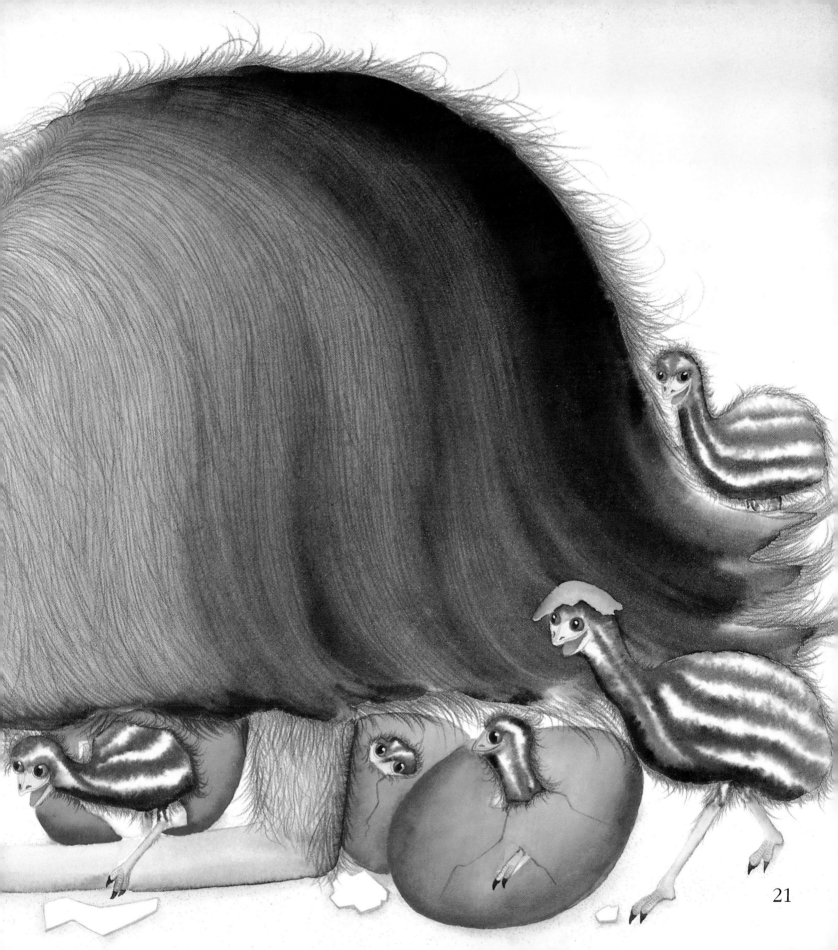

21

Enoch had to show someone his new family,
so he tidied the nest
before setting off down the path
to the Emu Club
with the babies following.
1 2 3 4 5 6 7 8 9

"Look at my new babies, boys,"
he said to his friends,
as they stood drinking at the billabong.
"All my own work. Well, er, nearly!"

The emus at the club were most impressed.
"Very fine young birds, very fine," they said,
"and well-behaved, too. Fine, fine, very fine."
And they all bent down to look at Enoch's babies.

Emu Club

24

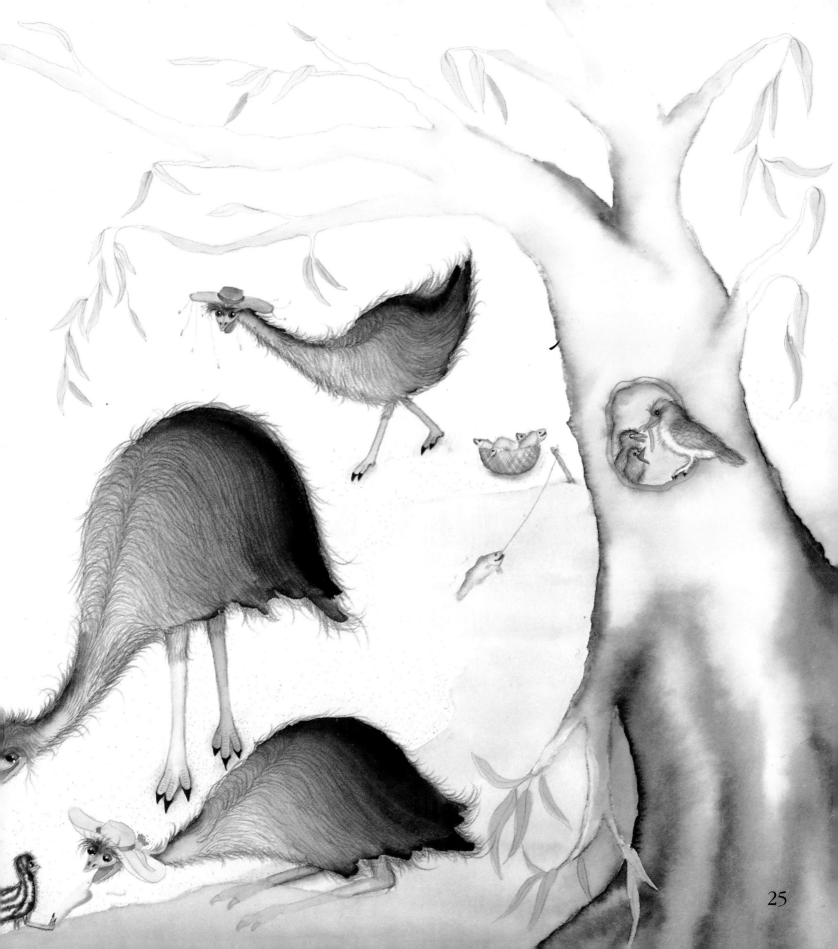

All, that is, except Eben, an uppity young emu
who was silly enough to give a little chuckle
at the sight of Enoch with his chicks.

But not for long,
because Enoch's eyes started to blaze,
and his kicking toe started to twitch.

"Um, yes, now you come to think of it,"
said Eben suddenly. "Fine, fine, very fine.
Never thought of raising babies myself.
Might give it a go."

27

"Quite, quite," said all the others.
"Seems a fitting thing to do.
We might try too."

And indeed they did.
Next season all the male emus
came to the Emu Club with their chicks.
And would you believe it,
they have done so ever since!

28

Partly True Tales — this part is true . . .

The story you have read about Enoch the Emu is make-believe. It is called a fantasy. However, part of it is true.

Emu fathers, found in Australia, really do sit on the nest until the chicks hatch and then care for their young. For most other kinds of birds, it is the mother who hatches the eggs and takes care of the newborn birds. Some other father birds care for their young. Here are a few from around the world.

Phalarope fathers sit on the eggs while their wives chase away rivals. They can be found in Alaska and Canada.

Ostrich fathers have several wives, and they do their part in guarding all the eggs. They live in Africa.

Pheasant-tailed jacana fathers build nests where the mother bird lays four eggs and flies away, leaving the father to incubate the brood. They live in India, Asia, and the Philippines.

Quetzal fathers take their turn protecting the eggs and feeding their young. They may be found in Mexico and Central America.

Penguin fathers nest a single egg between their feet and stop eating for the three months it takes to hatch the egg. They are found in Antarctica.

31

NOT AR

Library of Congress Cataloging-in-Publication Data
Winch, Gordon, 1930-
  Enoch, the emu.
  Originally published: Adelaide : Childerset, 1986.
  Summary: As Emus really do, Enoch sits on the nest for weeks till the nine eggs
laid by his wife hatch, and then he proudly shows his babies off to his friends at
the Emu Club.
  [1. Emus--Fiction. 2. Animals--Habits and behavior--Fiction. 3. Australia--
Fiction] I. Gristwood, Doreen, 1959-   ill. II. Title.
PZ7.W7218En 1988 [E]   88-42924
ISBN 1-55532-908-X

North American edition first published in 1988 by

Gareth Stevens, Inc.
7317 West Green Tree Road
Milwaukee, Wisconsin 53223, USA

1 2 3 4 5 6 7 8 9 93 92 91 90 89 88